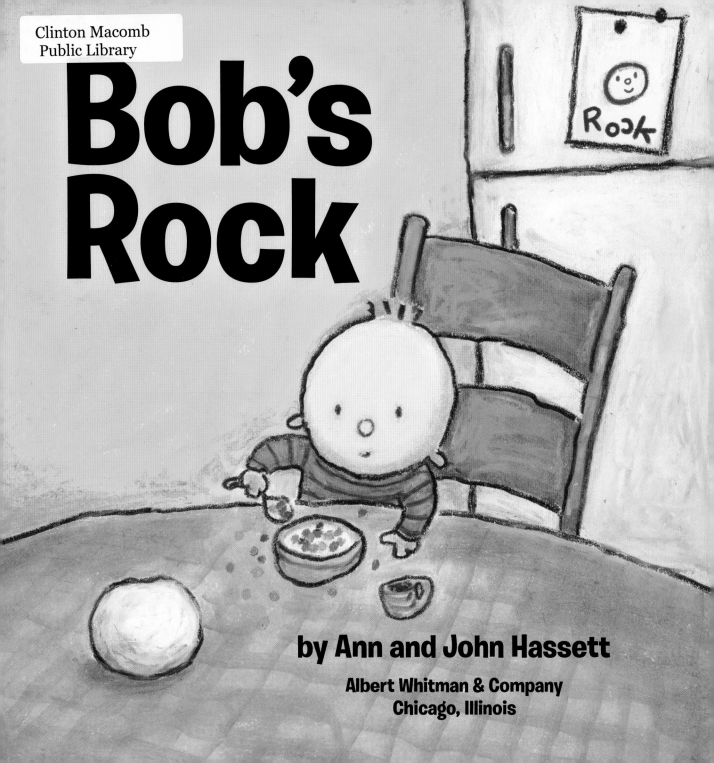

Bob's Rock

by Ann and John Hassett

Albert Whitman & Company
Chicago, Illinois

For Kate and Elizabeth
—AH and JH

Library of Congress Cataloging-in-Publication
data is on file with the publisher.

Text copyright © 2017 by Ann Hassett and John Hassett
Pictures copyright © 2017 by John Hassett
Published in 2017 by Albert Whitman & Company
ISBN 978-0-8075-0672-1

Printed in China
10 9 8 7 6 5 4 3 2 1 LP 22 21 20 19 18 17

Design by Jordan Kost

For more information about Albert Whitman & Company,
visit our website at www.albertwhitman.com.

Max has a dog.

Bob has a rock.

"Dog will do tricks," said Max.

"Rock will do tricks," said Bob.

"Sit," said Max.

Dog did not sit.

"Rock sits," said Bob.

"Stay," said Max.

Dog did not stay.

"Rock stays," said Bob.

"Fetch," said Max.

Dog did not fetch.

"Rock fetches," said Bob.

"Jump," said Max.

Dog did not jump.

"Rock jumps," said Bob.

"Roll over," said Max.

Dog did not roll over.

"Rock rolls over," said Bob.

"Speak," said Max.

Dog did not speak.

"Rock speaks," said Bob.

"Max stepped in dog poo," said Rock.

Bob put Rock in his pocket.

Rock had a nap.

Bark